The Canadian Adventures of

ANGUS

AND

EDMOND

Written by Gunna Dickson

With Illustrations by Judi Bradford

The Canadian Adventures of Angus and Edmond

Published by Gunna Dickson
25 Tudor City Place
New York, NY 10017
www.gdicksonbooks.com

Text copyright ©2021 by Gunna Dickson
Illustration copyright ©2021 by Judi Bradford

ISBN (hardcover): 978-0-578-98196-3

For Wee Geoffrey

CHAPTER 1
New York City

Pine garlands and red velvet bows adorned the wrought iron fences around the small Tudor parks, bringing a festive air to the neighborhood. Angus surveyed the scene from the windowsill on the 17th floor of their New York City high-rise. He had an idea.

He jumped down and crossed the living room, where Edmond was watching TV.

"Edmond! Where is our globe?"

"Uh... I dunno, Angus..." Edmond lied. "Did you look in the closet?"

"I'm looking now, but I don't see it. It was always right here... but now it's not."

"Hmmm, can't imagine what could have happened to it," Edmond mumbled, pretending to be engrossed in the nightly news.

Angus rummaged around some more for the inflatable globe they kept folded neatly along with their other possessions, but finally gave up. He closed the closet door and sat down next to his brother on the living room couch.

"So, what's new in the world?

"Nothing much…"

"Really? Looks like crime is rising, people are getting sick, drugs are coming across the border. What's wrong with you? You're acting funny, bro."

"What do you mean?"

"That's *exactly* what I mean. Suddenly you don't know anything. I know you better than that. Are you sure you don't know what happened to our globe?"

Edmond shrugged his narrow shoulders.

"*Edmond…?!?!*"

"All right, I'll tell you, but promise you won't get mad?"

Eyes narrowed, Angus stared hard at his little brother.

The Angora-mix littermates were nearly identical with soft white coats, round golden eyes, pink noses and pink paw pads. But Angus was a few minutes older and had the weight advantage.

The holidays brought a festive air to the neighborhood.

3

With a loud sigh of resignation, Edmond jumped off the couch and walked to the closet. He reached way back into the farthest corner and pulled out the tightly folded globe he had hidden away after their return from Budapest and the close call in Vienna.

He tossed it to Angus, who took a step forward, his ears flattening against his head and tail getting bushy. Just then the doorbell buzzed.

"Saved by the bell!" said Edmond, nimbly sidestepping his bigger brother. "I'll go see who it is!"

Standing in the carpeted hallway were their friends and neighbors Lulu and Valentina. Lulu was president of the Tudor Adopted Animals Club. The spunky little

Jack Russell terrier was wearing a knit designer vest with silvery threads running through it, and Valentina's sleek black coat and natural white bib were offset by a red lacquered collar with a rhinestone buckle. Each was holding a plate of cookies.

Lulu held her platter out in front of her.

"These are for you! Elaine baked them. They're still warm!" she said.

"And these are from Rebecca!" said Valentina, paws outstretched. "We've already dropped off cookies for Harry and Helen, Scotch and Susan, TJ, Violet, Jack and RJ, and Mangolito and Eva. We saved you for last!"

"What a nice surprise!" Edmond took a step back, inhaling the delicious aroma. "Come on in, girls! The Dicksons are out for the evening."

The apartment was warm and cheerful. A Christmas tree stood atop a small round table in the corner of the living room near the windows. Topped by a white ceramic kitty angel, its branches were adorned with multi-colored lights and a variety of ornaments, including one from the White House as well as a string of green carnival beads from a Key West parade.

"Let's have a holiday picnic!" Lulu and Valentina exclaimed in unison.

"What a good idea!" Edmond was quick to agree, welcoming any distraction that would put off having to face his brother's ire.

To protect the Oriental style carpet, the four friends spread out one of the quilts made by their friend Buddy's mom, Donna, in Tucker, Georgia, and laid out a picnic spread of cookies and milk.

"Chocolate chip cookies are Elaine's specialty. What makes them unique is that she rolls out the dough and uses cookie cutters, then puts different color icing on them," said Lulu proudly pointing to silver bells, gold stars and red-and-green striped candy canes.

"And Rebecca's friends say her lightly glazed soft gingerbread cookies are so good they should be sold in Bloomingdale's," boasted Valentina.

They all formed a small circle and the lively chatter soon turned to their previous travel adventures in Scotland, Florida, Spain, Italy and Hungary.

"Don't forget Vienna!" said Valentina. "The shopping was divine, and the sightseeing, the waltz lessons. What fun!"

"... until we had to spend the night locked in the Volksgarten..." Angus interrupted, glancing at Lulu.

The little dog stiffened and turned her face away, lifting her chin in quiet defiance.

"Angus, no!" Edmond cut off his brother, sensing that Angus was about to blame Lulu for the mishap that almost caused them to remain in Austria and look for new owners. "Be fair; it was nobody's fault."

"Anyway, we're all here now -- safe at home." Valentina deftly changed the subject. "Say, are you boys planning another trip?"

"Angus wants to, but I'm not sure..." said Edmond.

"Well, we don't have to travel far. I was thinking we'd pay a quick visit to our neighbors to the North."

"You mean the 18th floor, Angus?"

"No, bro, I was thinking Canada."

* * *

The Plan

When the girls left, Angus folded the quilt and put it back in the closet. He reached inside one of the Sherpa pet carriers there and took out a colorful tile. To celebrate the lads' good fortune of being adopted by the Dicksons, the New York Humane Society employees wanted to give them a farewell present and the brothers specifically asked for the tile they had found on the office wall.

Unaware of its significance, the staff was happy to wrap it up in tissue paper for them. They did not know the tile had special powers that enabled the boys to use the concept of time-travel. It was patterned after a TV series their caretakers liked to watch – a magical story about an English lady who touched a large flat standing stone in the Scottish Highlands and was transported back in time. In the blink of an eye, the lads could enter a time warp.

CHAPTER 2
Montreal

The morning sky was a cloudless, frosty blue when the lads boarded the plane. Angus tightened his seatbelt, put their phone in Airplane Mode and accessed his free Duolingo app.

Before their trip, he had engaged a private tutor to help freshen up his French language skills. Natasha of Larchmont was not only beautiful, she was an excellent teacher and gently patient with Angus' pronunciation issues. He would try his best not to let her down.

"Mon Dieu!" he muttered. "I sure hope that Canadians are more tolerant than the French!"

Edmond inserted his earbuds and closed his eyes.

It was a short flight -- 1 hour, 20 minutes -- from LaGuardia (LGA) to Pierre Elliott Trudeau International Airport (YUL).

Everything at YUL was DIY. The brothers processed their own arrival forms at individual kiosks and cleared customs with minimal contact. On the lower level were vending machines that dispensed OPUS smart cards that allowed them to use public transport in Greater

Montreal and Quebec City. They had done their research and knew that the 747 bus line had 24/7 service from the airport to downtown Montreal and stopped near their pet-friendly hotel on Saint-Antoine Street West. As prepared as they could be, they left the terminal and joined the travelers queuing for the next bus.

The driver, a tall red-haired woman, skillfully guided the vehicle along the Autoroute 20. The lads looked out the window at the stark landscape of flat stretches of snow-covered land, with simple box-like buildings at the roadside. Angus listened intently to the other passengers conversing in French. After a half-hour ride, the brothers hopped off the bus at the fifth stop, on René Lévesque Boulevard.

"René Lévesque was the 23rd Premier of Quebec," Angus explained as they walked down the steep hill to Viger Avenue. "He founded the Parti Québécois and was the first to try to get political independence for Quebec."

They turned left at Victoria Square, a plaza with trees and benches. After a recent snowfall, gravel had been scattered liberally on the sidewalks and the tiny pebbles hurt the lads' soft paw-pads and caught in the wheels of the midnight blue BRIC's Milano rolling duffel bag they had acquired during their trip to Italy.

As they proceeded along the square, they saw a building with a liveried doorman and, just to be sure they were on the right track, stopped to ask directions.

"*Excusez moi, Meowsieur. Où est la Rue Saint-Antoine Ouest?*" said Angus, pronouncing Saint Antoine *Sant* Antoine.

"Ah, **Saint** Antoine. *Marcher tout droit,*" the doorman replied helpfully, pointing straight ahead.

"*Merci, Meowsieur,*" Angus nodded politely, then turned to Edmond.

"French Canadians speak differently from the way the French do in France," he noted. "I appreciate that they also speak more slowly and seem more friendly."

The lads made another left turn and walked for several blocks until they reached their hotel. Inside they took an escalator up to the lobby, where they were greeted at the front desk by Marco. He checked them in and handed them the room key card along with a folded paper map of *Vieux Montréal*.

"Your room is ready, if you'd like to go up. Take the elevator to the 10th floor. It's just there, to your right."

As the doors closed, the boys heard a pleasant recorded voice say: "*Rez-de-chaussée, on monte,*" making Angus grin from ear to ear. "I am going to like it here, Edmond. Somehow 'Ground floor, going up' sounds a lot better in French!"

CHAPTER 3
Montreal

The boys unpacked and arranged their things neatly in the hotel room closet. They were eager to explore and savor the flavors of "the most European city in North America." To walk its cobblestone streets and wide plazas and parks. To see its ornate fountains and grand architecture, look in the display windows of its fashionable boutiques, and taste its cuisine.

They left the hotel by the back way, passing the business center and entering an elevated walkway that led them across an indoor shopping mall to an adjacent building and out onto Rue Saint-Jacques.

"Aah, *regarde*, Edmond, *la Vieille Ville*... look, the Old Town. See how the modern buildings co-exist with architecture from the 1800s? It's quite magical, *n'est-ce pas*? Isn't that so?"

At the corner of Rue Saint-Pierre, Angus pointed to an impressive four-story sandstone structure with granite columns and tall chimneys. "That's the Old Molson Bank Building. It was founded by the sons of the brewery and steamship magnate, John Molson, and its headquarters opened in 1866. At the time, this street was the financial center of Canada. The faces of the three men carved above the front door represent the founder and his sons, and the sculpture up high in the center is the family coat of arms. *C'est magnifique*, eh?"

Edmond nodded.

The brothers continued along Notre-Dame Street West – or *Rue Notre-Dame Ouest*, as Angus insisted on calling it. He was in his element, reading out loud all the street signs and store names in the historic district.

At Place d'Armes they came to the stately gray stone Notre-Dame Basilica, with two towers. They pulled on the handles of its heavy wooden doors and paused inside to purchase tickets.

As they entered the 17th Century Catholic cathedral, they were awe-struck by the blue lit, gleaming gold grandeur of its interior. The soaring ceilings, large stained-glass windows, deep blue pointed arches, ribbed vaults, stars, painted columns and burnished wood-carved balconies stimulated their senses. A 20-minute guided tour was included in the price of admission and they hurried over to join a tour in progress.

The thundering chords of the massive pipe organ shook them from head to toe as they sat with the group, exchanging wide-eyed looks.

They were awestruck by the 17th Century cathedral.

"That magnificent sound is coming from our Casavant Freres organ, which dates back to 1891," their guide said. "It is 32 feet high, has four keyboards, 92 stops and 7,000 individual pipes."

"Aaaah-h-h" the group chorused. As they moved along slowly, the guide continued: "You may find it unusual that the stained-glass windows here do not depict biblical scenes but scenes from the religious history of Montreal," he said, pausing to allow the visitors to look around to confirm and absorb the information.

"It is also worthy of note that we have two Canadian saints named Marguerite," he said. "Marguerite Bourgeoys, who grew up in France, was declared the first female saint of Canada by Pope John Paul II. Her legacy was to empower women, children and the poor through education.

And Marguerite d'Youville, named "mother of Universal Charity" by Pope John XXIII, became the first Canadian-born saint when she was canonized in 1990."

The boys exchanged glances as they listened.

"The sanctuary was completed in 1830, and the basilica has been the site of many special events, including the state funeral for our prime minister and a concert by Luciano Pavarotti, the Italian opera singer."

The guide asked them to take seats in a section of the front pews.

"Celine Dion, the French-Canadian singing star was married in this church," he said. "And some years later, sadly, the funeral of her husband, Rene Angelil, also took place here."

He looked at Edmond and smiled. "You are sitting exactly where she sat. So, maybe from now on you will sing beautifully."

The other tourists tittered as Edmond's nose and ears turned a brighter shade of pink.

Before the group disbanded, they were urged to experience Aura, a sound-and-light spectacle that showcases the basilica's extraordinary beauty.

"I promise you, it stirs the soul," said the guide.

Merci beaucoup!" said the brothers appreciatively.

As they walked back to the hotel, Edmond was pensive

and tested his voice, softly humming Celine Dion's hit love song *Pour que tu m'aimes encore* while Angus continued to point out signs and advertisements, reading the messages out loud.

Soon he felt a tap on his shoulder.

"Angus, how do you say 'That's enough' in French?" Edmond asked innocently.

"Well, you could say *c'est assez*. Or a stronger expression might be *Ça suffit!*"

"*ÇA SUFFIT*, Angus!" Edmond shouted.

"All right, all right, keep your fur on, bro," Angus said defensively. A self-proclaimed citizen of the world, he was unapologetic about trying to fit in wherever they traveled.

The brothers walked the rest of the way in silence.

CHAPTER 4
Montreal

Gusts of wind buffeted sparse white flakes in the chilly air as the boys set off for the waterfront and the streets and quays of the historic Old Port.

Snow was collecting on the toques and shoulders of Montrealers hurrying to work and visitors pausing to consult their maps. It drew bright white outlines on bare brown branches, and added a touch of sparkle to the already decorative rooftops.

"This is so pretty," said Edmond, sticking out his tongue to catch the flakes.

"Did you know that each snowflake is unique... no two are the same!" Angus offered.

"I'll take your word for it, bro."

There was much to see along the 1.5 mile-long stretch of the Promenade du Vieux Port, with four quays jutting out into the St. Lawrence river, where ice-breakers were laboring to clear shipping lanes.

The Old Port offered many recreational activities as well as restaurants, shops and entertainment venues. The Grand Quai and its international cruise terminal, fittingly was located opposite the Pointe-à-Callière museum, where immigrants arrived at the turn of the 20th Century. Today it welcomes cruise ships and thousands of visitors from all parts of the world.

Angus pointed across the Alexandra Basin. "Look, Edmond. See that odd looking structure? That's Habitat 67 -- a housing complex built for Expo 67 world's fair as an example of future apartment living."

"Hmmm... it looks like a lot of boxes," Edmond said thoughtfully. "Very appealing."

Walking briskly, the lads came to Quai King-Edward, the site of the IMAX theater and Montreal Science Center. Then, squinting into the snow, they passed Quai Jacques Cartier, where the Cirque du

Soleil thrilled audiences with its grand shows. They were on a mission as they forged ahead toward the blurry outline of the biggest ferris wheel in Canada.

Finally, the boys arrived at the Quai de l'Horloge, and the Bonsecours Basin Skating Rink at the foot of the 200-foot-high La Grande Roue.

They rented skates and after a wobbly start, settled into a cautious rhythm, staying within reach of each other in case one of them stumbled or fell. Across the river they could see the lower tip of Ile Sainte Helene, the site of the Montreal Biosphere. The museum devoted to the environment had originally been the United States Pavilion at Expo 67.

After a while Angus called a time out, skating over to the edge of the rink. He decided to stretch his leg muscles, not realizing a skater was approaching fast. The skater did a skillful evasive maneuver worthy of Canadian hockey star Sidney Crosby, then circled back toward the boys, stopping short in front of them, spraying them with ice shavings.

"*C'est quoi ton problème?* You almost caused an accident!" a dark-haired woman shouted. Then, seeing the boys' horrified faces, she softened her tone.

"Are you visitors?" she asked.

"*Oui, Mademeowselle,*" Angus said shakily.

"*Venez avec moi,*" the woman said, stifling a smile. "Come with me." She led them to a low wall next to the Grande Roue and they all sat down.

"*Je m'excuse.* My apologies. I am Aline and I'm happy to see you are enjoying my city," she said, shaking the snow off her dark curls.

"Oh, yes. We love Montreal," the boys said in unison, then introduced themselves.

Aline continued: "This rink is very popular. Open more than 100 days a year, it's a good place for beginners like yourselves because the ice is of very high quality," she said. "The venue is lit up in the evening and has a musical theme -- Classical Monday, French Sunday or Romantic Thursday. Try to find time to take a ride on La Grande Roue. On a clear day the view is marvelous and the cabins are nice and warm in winter."

"Perhaps you could recommend a place for dinner tonight, Aline?" asked Angus.

"Ah, there are so many excellent places to eat in this area... let me think. Hmmm... I really like the restaurants in the William Gray Hotel. It's not far from here. I might join you, if I can clear my schedule."

"That would be awesome," Angus said. "It's always good to make a new friend. Edmond and I have friends all over the world."

After a wobbly start, they settled into a cautious rhythm.

* * *

For the walk back to their hotel, the boys chose the cozy protection of the narrow Saint-Paul Street, with its picturesque buildings and shops. The snow was getting deeper.

Ferry lights, pine boughs and velvet bows framed shop windows and adorned roof contours as they walked past the domed Marché Bonsecours and Place Jacques-Cartier. Clusters of street lanterns illuminated holiday decorations – sleds, elves and trees.

"Oh, my, it's so pretty, isn't it, Edmond?" Angus looked to his right, but his brother wasn't there.

"Edmond? ... Edmond?!"

"Down here, Angus..."

Angus followed his brother's voice and saw Edmond lying on his back in a snowdrift on the street.

"What are you doing down there?!"

"I was so busy looking around, I didn't see the curb at the intersection. I think I twisted my foot..." Edmond said, wincing.

Angus swooped down to help him and looked concerned as Edmond tried gingerly to put his weight on his left hind paw.

"Ow!" he cried out and nearly lost his footing again on the slick cobblestones.

As the brothers continued along the street. Edmond's limp was getting more pronounced.

They came to a shop with an enticing window display of winter scenes and maple syrup treats. The sign above the door said Délices Érable & Cie.

"Let's go in," said Edmond. "I need to sit down."

Inside the tastefully decorated shop were a myriad maple and honey products – syrup, ice cream, pastries, confectionery and marinades. So many things to look at, and some of them to sample. They ordered maple lattes and hungrily eyed the range of locally sourced products.

They soon had a second wind, but Edmond's foot was throbbing.

"We will be back!" they vowed.

Leaning on Angus, Edmond limped back to their hotel, where Marco assured them an ice pack would be sent up *tout de suite*. Right away.

That night it was room service for the boys. Angus called the restaurant to cancel their dinner reservation using his best French. "*Voici Meowsieur Dickson. Je suis vraiment désolé d'annuler notre réservation pour ce soir. Oh, et veuillez envoyer nos regrets à Mademeowselle Aline.*" Mr. Dickson here. I am truly sorry we must cancel our reservation for tonight. And please give our regrets to Mademoiselle Aline.

Then, with a sigh of resignation, he punched the room service key. "One order of Salmon and Risotto, *s'il vous plaît*, with two plates and two sets of cutlery. *Merci, Madame!*"

CHAPTER 5

The snow was falling steadily as Angus wrapped a Canada scarf around his neck and pulled his brand new red toque with white maple leaf over his ears. It was clear Edmond was in no shape to do any touring, so Angus decided to go it alone.

"Get some rest, *mon frère*," Angus said with a wave. "*À bientôt!*"

Edmond put a Do Not Disturb sign on the door and hobbled over to a cabernet-colored padded armchair. Picking up a fresh bag of ice, he propped up his injured

paw on a pillow and settled in to watch TV.

Angus took the long escalator from the lobby down to street level, where several taxis were waiting. He jumped in the first one and told the driver.

"Au Mont Royal, s'il vous plait!"

"Bien Sur! Vous voulez faire du ski? Luge? Patinage?"

"Uh, no. Not today. I'd like to get an aerial view of the city. I've heard it is amazing, and you can also get hot chocolate."

"Well, *Monsieur*, I must tell you honestly that today is not a good day for that. Visibility is very poor."

"Ah, *oui*, of course," Angus looked dejected.

"But wait, I have an idea... and it involves hot chocolate. Afterwards I will take you wherever you'd like to go."

"Sounds like a plan!" Angus accepted enthusiastically.

* * *

An hour later, the taxi dropped Angus off at the corner of Rue de Bleury and Avenue du President Kennedy, near the Black Watch of Canada Armoury. The brothers were enormously proud of their Scottish heritage, and right after a Mount Royal aerial view, the

Royal Highland Regiment's museum was next on Angus' list of things to see.

As he approached the armory doors, he stopped. The Coordinator of the Museum and Archives had posted a notice. It read: "The museum is closed for renovations. We will remain closed until restrictions regarding access to the building are lifted."

Strike two. Now Angus was truly dejected.

Shielding his eyes from the driving snow, he trudged through the drifts along Rue Sainte Catherine, until he came upon an entrance to *La ville souterraine* and Place Ville Marie shopping mall. It wasn't that he liked to shop. His paws, nose and ears were cold, and he wanted to go underground to escape the harsh wind.

As he walked through the vast complex, looking in shop windows, he saw an arrow pointing to the *Observatoire*. Things were starting to look up – quite literally. He took the elevator to the 46th floor. And Fortune smiled on him.

The flurries had subsided and the powerful wind had parted the clouds, allowing the sun to break through. For about 15 minutes, safe and warm behind a glass wall, Angus was able to enjoy an aerial view of Montreal. He admired the snowclad cityscape and tried to picture what it would look like in the summer. He conjured a city decked out in lush shades of green. Then he imagined how the downtown area would appear in the evening, with a setting sun, then with city lights ablaze against a midnight sky. What a glorious sight!

But, in the end, he was glad his first visit was on a winter's day, when every detail was clearly visible for him to see and appreciate.

On his way out, Angus bought a stretchy bandage

for Edmond's paw and stopped in the Place Ville Marie gourmet food hall to pick up hot chocolate and a *baguettine* with ham and cheese, cut in half. Staying underground, he soon found himself in the train station, where he purchased two round trip tickets. Back at street level, he hurried back to the hotel.

The wind had closed up the clouds again and the snow stuck to his fur. He arrived in the lobby looking like a snowman with a bushy tail.

"*C'est toi, Monsieur Angus?*" asked Marco.

"*C'est moi,*" Angus grunted as he headed for the elevator.

* * *

The sound of the door lock clicking open awakened Edmond from his nap. He had tried watching TV, but nearly all the programs were in French and he had dozed off.

"I'm back!" Angus said cheerily, shaking the wet snow off his toque and scarf. "I must say I had an interesting day."

He unwrapped the *baguettine*, handed half to Edmond, along with a luke-warm cup of chocolate, and hopped up on the comfortable king-size bed.

"I took notes, so I wouldn't leave anything out," Angus

said, opening his tartan notebook. "Ah, here we are – Mount Royal!"

"The taxi driver took me part of the way up. At Beaver Lake Pavilion you can get hot chocolate and watch the skaters. There are lots of winter activities there. Altogether, Mount Royal Park has 14 miles of trails for activities such as cross-country skiing and slopes for snowboarding and sledding.

"But you know what I took away from it most of all, Edmond? Here, people of all ages have a real love and appreciation for outdoor recreation! Any time of year. And the park is just minutes from the city center."

Angus told of seeing skaters twirling on the rink and among the trees at picturesque Beaver Lake, and described the snow tubing lanes and well-marked hiking trails.

"The taxi driver said that, on a clear night, you can take a snowshoe trek through the forest and see the city lights. And that's not all. I'll bet you don't know who designed Mount Royal Park!"

"I'll bet I don't," said Edmond, chewing a small piece of ham.

"It was Frederick Law Olmsted, who also designed Central Park in New York City! And where do you think I went next?"

Safe and warm, Angus enjoyed an aerial view of Montreal.

Edmond looked up glumly from his sandwich.

"Well, that part was disappointing. The Black Watch Museum was closed for renovation. I had hoped it would be one of the highlights of my day.

"But then things got better again. I took refuge from the snow in Place Ville Marie, a business center and shopping mall that is connected to an entire underground city. There are more than a thousand stores, restaurants, office towers, theaters and hotels. Best of all, I got a brilliant view of the city from the observatory and was able to stay indoors nearly all the way home."

Angus paused, squinting at his notebook... "Hmmm, can't read my own writing here. It looks like chicken scratch." He chuckled "that's pretty funny considering I'm a cat, ha ha."

"Oh, yes, the underground network is about 20 miles long and it even connects with the Gare Central. I got us train tickets to Quebec City for tomorrow morning. How are you feeling anyway? Has the swelling gone down?"

"It's better, but still tender to walk on," Edmond replied. "I must say my biggest challenge has been the French language TV. The only English channel here is CNN."

Angus was indignant. "You can't expect to see any real news on CNN. Remember how dismissive they were about the vampire exclusive I called in from Budapest?"

Edmond nodded, popping the last morsel of *baguettine* in his mouth. "Listen, I had an interesting experience as well. A chatty hotel fellow named Englebert delivered my ice bags. He said his mother was a pop music fan and named him after the British singer Englebert Humperdinck. She also liked the Welsh singer Tom Jones, and named her second son Tom. Her third child was a girl but, guess what, if it had been a boy, Englebert said she would have named him Elvis!

"Isn't that funny, Angus?" Edmond giggled.

"Yes, Edmond," Angus stretched and stifled a yawn. He was having trouble staying awake. "By the way, our train leaves at 9."

Before turning off the light, he left instructions for an 8 a.m. wake-up call.

CHAPTER 6
Quebec City

Angus had a guide book on his lap, next to his tartan notebook. During the ride from Montreal's Central station to Quebec City, he was quickly filling up the pages with notes.

Three hours later, they stepped off the train into bright sunlight, made blinding by the glistening expanse of snow that blanketed the surroundings.

Edmond's paw was still a bit tender so the lads hired a horse-drawn carriage for a tour of the Old Town. The calèche was waiting for them at the station and would drop them off at their hotel at the edge of the Plains of Abraham. They figured the ride would also allow them to get their bearings in the picturesque, walled old-world city.

The lads clambered up onto the comfortable seats and settled in. The driver, a young man with dark hair and mischievous brown eyes, turned sideways and looked down at them from his perch. *"Bienvenue, mes amis!"* he said pleasantly.

They began their tour along the narrow winding streets of North America's first French city.

He was delighted to see Angus' face light up, but noting the expression on Edmond's face, he switched to English, which the boys learned could be increasingly rare in some parts of that beguiling town, where Quebecois nationalist feelings sometimes ran high. Those sentiments were reinforced by the ubiquitous blue-and-white fleur-de-lis flag and license plates with the motto *"Je me souviens."* I remember.

"My name is André," the driver said. "Welcome to the birthplace of French civilization in North America – *C'est beau, n'est-ce pas?* Beautiful, eh?"

"I am what people call a true native, or Québécois Pure Laine. As you say -- dyed-in-the-wool, which means my family can trace our lineage back to the original settlers who sailed from France in the 1600s. As your driver, it is my mission today to give you an unforgettable experience!"

And so began their tour, along narrow winding streets of North America's first French city, whose beauty was enhanced by holiday decorations arrayed against a snowy backdrop.

"Our little tour does not allow much time, so what highlights I cannot show you, I will try to tell you about," said André as the gentle caramel-colored horse with a white blaze on his forehead settled into a rhythmic trot.

"There are four gates to the *Vieille Ville*, which is the only walled city north of Mexico. In 1985, Old Quebec was proclaimed a World Heritage Site by UNESCO. And it is easy to see why they would want it to be preserved."

He stretched out his arm. "*Et là-bas* – over there – is the Old Port and *le fleuve* Saint-Laurent, the St. Lawrence River.

"I urge you to make time to visit Quartier Petit-Champlain, the oldest commercial street in North America and an enchanting part of our city. There are many interesting shops and galleries. You are sure to find just what you are looking for there."

One by one, André drew their attention to points of interest like the Museum of Civilization, Montmorency Park, Place Royale, Place d'Armes, Fairmont Le Chateau Frontenac, La Citadelle de Quebec and Parliament Hill.

The conversation between André and Angus was gradually shifting to French, but Edmond didn't mind. He was content to absorb the scenic beauty of the surroundings, the picturesque cobbled streets and historic monuments and homes dating back to the 17th and 18th centuries. All of it made even more magical by the fairydust-like coating of sparkling snow.

Edmond decided to amuse himself. Mindful of the Basilica guide's prediction about his voice, and inspired by the steady hoofbeats, he began drumming his front paws on the thick blanket that covered their laps and sang to the tune of Jingle Bells:

"Dashing through the snow
In a one-horse vieux calèche, eh?
O'er the Plains we go
Laughing all the way... ha ha ha..."

He chuckled, pleased with himself for adapting the lyrics to their Canadian surroundings.

"Well done, *Monsieur* Edmond," said André, placing the reins over his forearm and using both hands to applaud.

"*Regardez*," he pointed toward the Parliament Building. "Imagine, in just over a month it will be Quebec Winter Carnival, and right there a life-size storybook Ice Palace will become the centerpiece of a magnificent display of sound and light. Over a hundred elaborate snow and ice sculptures will be built all around the city – dragons, bears, exotic faces, winged

creatures and even model cities. There will be night parades, ice canoe races and so much more..."

"Oh, yes," Angus chimed in and read from his notes. "The jolly likeness of Bonhomme Carnaval will beam from under his holly-red stocking cap. Best described as a snowman with legs, the mascot's image will appear on T-shirts and a multitude of souvenirs."

"You are right, *mon ami*. But in the flesh, or costume, there is only one Bonhomme and he is guest of honor at all Carnival functions."

Angus and Edmond's imaginations were in overdrive and André's enthusiasm was contagious.

"You will see revelers bundled up in furs and parkas, wearing a fringed red Carnival sash around the waist. Some will steady themselves with bright-red plastic walking canes, occasionally raising them to their lips."

The brothers exchanged puzzled looks.

"The canes are hollow, *mes amis*, but they are not empty," André adopted a conspiratorial tone. "They contain caribou -- a potent, tasty mix of spirits. It's made from spiced rum, gin, syrup and hot water."

"And, for a special meal, I suggest you try Poutine, the provincial dish of Quebec. It consists of only three ingredients – French fries and cheese curds, covered with gravy," said André, adding with a laugh: "Actually, in Quebec the word is slang for mess."

"What's most amusing is that while it started out as a poor-man's dish, it has gained acceptance in many circles. One can now order Foie gras poutine, braised beef poutine, and even lobster poutine."

After several more travel tips and suggestions, André announced:

"*Et voilà!* We are at the Plains of Abraham, and here is your hotel." He pulled back on the reins, bringing the calèche to a halt at the entrance. The three exchanged hugs and the lads waved goodbye.

"*Au revoir! Merci beaucoup!*"

CHAPTER 7
Quebec City

Early the next morning, Edmond flexed his paw and found it a little less stiff. Just to be safe though, Angus helped him wrap it with the stretchy bandage.

From their hotel window they watched smoke rising from chimneys, looking like frozen white columns in the frigid air. The sun's rays, congealed in a tight orange halo, managed to throw off enough light to transform the ice-clogged St. Lawrence into flowing molten gold.

"This is what they call the *froid carnivalesque*," Angus shivered. "Brr-r-r-r."

"Let's treat ourselves to lunch at the Chateau Frontenac and go tobogganing. We'll make this a very special day. Our train back to Montreal leaves at 6."

They grabbed a couple of Beaver Tails and made their way to Quartier Petit-Champlain.

"Hee, hee, I can't wait to tell our friends we ate Beaver Tails for breakfast," Edmond giggled. "We won't tell them they are made of fried pastry dough."

The Quartier Petit-Champlain was truly an embarrassment of riches. There were shops selling interesting handmade products, boots, hats, gloves and jewelry. Imaginative eateries -- a Crêperie, a Fudgerie and a Nougaterie -- a theater, art gallery, elegant boutiques and souvenir shops. Edmond carefully selected a few special portable items, some with fleur-de-lis designs as souvenirs for friends.

To leave the Lower Town Angus had almost persuaded Edmond to take *L'Escalier Casse-Cou*, until he learned it meant "Breakneck Staircase." So they bypassed what Edmond called the Scary Stairs and rode the funicular up the steep incline to the Upper Town.

Alighting on the wide riverside Dufferin Terrace, the boys found themselves at the foot of one of the most spectacular buildings they had ever seen -- the clifftop Fairmont *Le Château Frontenac*.

"We need to take a selfie to send to Lulu and Valentina," said Angus. "They will be so jealous!"

"Yes, and then let's have lunch, and afterwards we can do the toboggan ride," Edmond suggested.

In the *Château* lobby they were enveloped in regal tones of dazzling gold and rich river blue. Indeed, the hotel welcomed royalty and heads of state -- kings and princesses, presidents and prime ministers. The boys felt a little out of their depth, but relaxed when they learned that pets were also welcome.

Their hearts were set on trying Poutine and they found it on the menu at the bistro, where a wall of windows with sheer curtains offered a view of the St. Lawrence. Angus took a deep breath and ordered: *"Poutine a la joue de boeuf effilochee... pour deux, s'il vous plaît"* -- for two please.

"Edmond, who would believe we are sitting in a fancy chateau, eating shredded beef cheek poutine with cheese and meat juice sauce and pickles! I've *got* to tell Jamie," Angus grabbed the phone and speed-dialed Inverness in Scotland.

Their former owner, Jamie MacBean, was a kind Scottish businessman who had dropped them off at the New York Humane Society when his company recalled him to the United Kingdom, where pets were required to be kept in quarantine.

As soon as Jamie picked up the phone, Angus couldn't contain his excitement.

"Jamie, you'll never, ever guess where we are!"

Angus regaled Jamie with their adventures so far. He urged Jamie and Wilbur T, their host in Key West, to visit Quebec City for Winter Carnival and suggested that Ian Hamilton ask Chef Morag to add Poutine to

the menu at Vine Leaf restaurant in St Andrews – with a Scottish twist, of course.

There was no time for dessert. Time was flying and the boys headed for the nearly 300-feet high toboggan run at one end of Terrace Dufferin.

The lads pulled the toboggan up the side of the slide and took their spot at the top of one of three icy 165-yard-long tubes. The panoramic view -- the ice-clogged St. Lawrence to the right and Le *Château* Frontenac straight ahead – was breathtaking.

The sled began its descent, hurtling down the steep slope toward the finish line at nearly 40 miles an hour, and the brothers clung to each other, screaming at the top of their lungs. What a thrill!

Safely back on Dufferin Terrace, the lads cast a long farewell look at the *Château* Frontenac. It was time to go to their own hotel and get ready for the trip back. As they hurried toward the Plains of Abraham, they stopped for maple taffy, a simple local dessert that involves only a wooden stick, snow and maple syrup.

It was late afternoon and, in December, darkness was not far away.

It was starting to snow again as they stood on the Plains. Once the site of a bloody battle, it was now a beautiful park with trails and benches and cross-country skiing right in the heart of town.

"Angus, I can't believe we are standing on the battlefield where Canada's fate was decided, where in 1759 the British Army and Royal Navy fought against the French. Incredibly, the Battle of Quebec lasted only about an hour and was fought with fewer than 10,000 troops. Both generals, Wolfe and Montcalm, were mortally wounded. It's all hard to believe, isn't it?"

"Yes, Edmond, we are experiencing history here, walking in the footsteps of warriors -- the British troops who defeated the French army and Canadian militia."

As he spoke, Angus was inspired.

The sled began its descent, hurtling down the steep slope.

"Let's play war games!" He started running in circles, kicking up snow and tossing it in the air, screaming at the top of his lungs. He ran and played and shouted until he fell on the soft, thick layer of snow, exhausted. The wet snow was coming down harder.

Angus sat up and looked around for his brother. He looked toward the spot he had last seen Edmond but there was no one there. There was no Edmond.

He frowned and looked around the vast snow-clad Plains, as far as the eye could see.

"Edmond!... Edmo-o-o-nd... Edmo-o-o-o-ond!"

"What's up, bro?" came a voice from close up.

Angus jumped and turned in the direction of the sound.

"Edmond?"

"Yes?"

"I can hear you, but I can't see you..."

A snowball suddenly flew past Angus' head and he spun around. This time he saw a knit hat with a red maple leaf on it and long billowing red CANADA scarf, seemingly suspended in the air. Two round golden orbs suddenly lit up just under the hat as Edmond's eyes glowed in the gathering dusk. The form of his little brother slowly took shape in the wintry storm.

"Nice trick, bro!" Angus exclaimed. "I think you're onto something -- something big! I envision battalions of white cats on snowy terrain. The advantages of having a fierce and invisible feline army are limitless... we could make up the sixth branch of the military after the Space Force. We could be the Ghost Force!

"Let's work up a formal proposal for the President on the train ride back. And we'll copy the Prime Minister of Canada, of course."

As they collected their bags and left for the train station, *Je me souviens* took on new meaning for the lads. It was a visit they would remember.

CHAPTER 8
Montreal

Checkout time was at noon. Edmond's foot was much improved and he spent the morning dashing around the *Vieux Ville* to pick up souvenirs. He went to Saint Paul Street to buy maple syrup and assorted sweets, as well as souvenir maple leaf toques and knit scarves.

An hour and a half later, the brothers were back at YUL, at their gate in the departure lounge. They felt sad to leave this special place that was so close to their New York home, yet a world away. They would surely have to return. There was so much more ground to cover - 13 provinces and three territories.

The brothers agreed that Nova Scotia, Latin for "New Scotland," should be next on their list.

Angus was looking through some flyers he had picked up at a tourism stand and suddenly thrust one in his brother's face.

"Edmond, Edmond, the RCMP are recruiting!"

"What?"

"The Royal Canadian Mounted Police! You know, those smart looking fellows on horseback, with the bright red tunics, dark breeches with a yellow stripe and broad brimmed hats! Just think how handsome we would look in red!"

"Well, I've always admired horses. It would be very cool to enforce the law while riding around looking smart," Edmond said wistfully.

"It's worth a shot. We may have to delay our return home."

That caused Edmond to frown.

"What, exactly, are the qualifications we'd have to meet, bro?" he asked guardedly.

"Well, let's see. It says here 'the cadet program takes place at the training facility in Regina, Saskatchewan, and lasts for 26 weeks'."

"Go on..."

"It says 'training can be very intense'. Recruits should be able to run 5 km continuously. They will also have to eventually work their way up to 10 and 20 km continuously."

"Is that so..." Edmond looked pained.

"Uh... candidates will be expected to display proficiency in physical fitness as well as police sciences, driving, and firearms."

"Anything else?" he prodded.

"Must meet vision and hearing standards (check!), be aware of requirements for tattoos and jewelry (check!), be of good character (check!), proficient in English and/or French (check, sort of), possess a valid, unrestricted driver's license (can't check that one.)"

Edmond's frown deepened. "Is that all?"

"A typical day runs from 6 a.m. to 4:30 p.m."

"Hmm, that could be a problem. We are not early risers."

"On the plus side, the training program is free."

"I dunno, Angus. I am starting to see fewer pros than cons..."

"Uh-oh... it also says 'To apply as a police officer of the RCMP **you must** be a Canadian citizen'."

Edmond breathed a sigh of relief.

"I guess that does it then. Hey, it's time to board our flight," he hopped off the seat and helped Angus pull their bulging rolling duffel into the jetway.

During the flight back to LaGuardia, Edmond photo-shopped their faces onto the RCMP flyer and sent it out to his distribution list along with "Greetings from Canada!"

CHAPTER 9
New York

The lads loved snow, and it loved them – it followed them home. The night before their arrival, a storm had dropped two feet of the white stuff on Central Park and brought Manhattan traffic to a standstill.

Angus and Edmond were excited as they sat on the windowsill watching big fluffy flakes dancing in the air. The wind blew deep drifts against the fence of the little park down below and covered the windshields and rooftops of cars with a thick coating of white.

"Let's call Sassy and Savannah and tell them to meet us at the usual place," Angus directed Edmond.

The brothers ran as fast as they could to a little pocket park near the UNICEF offices. With shrubs and dark green cast iron tables and chairs, it was one of their favorite meeting places in the warm weather months.

Their friends Sassy and Savannah were already waiting, wagging their tails with excitement.

"Welcome back from Canada!" they said.

"Thanks! It was a wonderful trip," Angus said. "Hey, we've got a great game we learned up North."

"Oh, yes! We'll teach you. It's so much fun," Edmond

chimed in. "It's called *cache-cache*! Basically, we choose someone to be "it" and they close their eyes and count to 50 while the rest of us hide. Sassy, you're 'it'!"

Always a good sport, Sassy squeezed her eyes shut and began counting out loud. "One, two... three... four..."

Angus and Edmond motioned for Savannah, a Miniature American Eskimo with a luxurious white coat, to follow them. All three huddled together in plain sight amid the snowdrifts, only a couple of yards from Sassy, who was still counting.

"Be sure to close your eyes and cover your nose with your paws," Edmond instructed Savannah.

"48... 49... 50," said Sassy. "Now what?"

"Now you say *prêt ou pas, j'arrive,*" came Angus' disembodied voice.

"Pretty paws..." Sassy repeated as she opened her eyes and looked around. She was surrounded by white. Mounds of snow were everywhere and the swirling flakes stuck to her eyelashes, making it hard to see.

Shielding her eyes, she walked cautiously, avoiding the legs of the metal tables and chairs that were mostly covered by the deepening drifts.

Then as she turned to her right, Sassy saw a small light come on. She walked toward it. After a few steps, she bumped right into Savannah as she looked into one of Angus' glowing eyes.

"Oh, my! You were standing right in front of me, and I didn't see you... at least not until Angus peeked!"

"I know, I know. You were taking so long, I got curious," Angus tried to justify himself. Edmond frowned and grunted his displeasure.

"OK Savannah, it's your turn!"

"*Un, deux, trois...*" Savannah counted, putting her paws over her eyes as Angus, Edmond and Sassy scrambled to find a hiding place.

It had been easy to play the camouflage game with Savannah's dense white coat, but rust-colored Beagle-terrier mix Sassy presented a problem.

"There's only one thing we can do, Sassy," said Angus. "We need to cover you up. Quick, we don't have much time."

Sassy gave in and allowed the brothers to build a wall of snow around her.

Just then Ellie, a friendly Dapple Dachshund who also lived in the neighborhood, raced around the corner, stopping short when she saw the other animals.

"Shhhh..." Angus whispered. "Don't make a sound! We're playing a game. You need to hide."

Ellie nodded and let the boys cover her with snow.

Satisfied that Sassy and Ellie had become invisible, the brothers squeezed their eyes shut and huddled on either side, paws pressed over their pink noses.

"This time, *no peeking*, Angus!" Edmond admonished his brother.

"48... 49... *cinquante... j'arrive!* Here I come!" Savannah called out, pronouncing the French rr's perfectly. She and her kitty sister, Serene, came from a musical household. Their mom Susan had a collection of French music, and sing-alongs were encouraged. Susan, Savannah and Serene sang roundelays and three-part harmonies to such classics as *La Mer* and

La Vie en Rose. Serene's favorite was *Alouette*, a nursery rhyme about a little bird.

Angus made a mental note to order some French CDs to help with his pronunciation issues.

Taking her paws from her eyes, Savannah saw lengthening shadows on the white snow in front of her. To her left, snow and gray shadows. To the right, more of the same. She spun around, then walked slowly among the heaps of drifts. All was still. Where could they be?

She circled the little park three times, and still saw only snow and shadows. Her friends had sure found a good hiding place. Savannah was just starting to feel discouraged when she noticed that one of the snowbanks was trembling. Her ears perked up and she tilted her head to the left, then to the right as she tried to figure out what could be making it move like that.

As the snow began to quake, she leapt backward.

"Ah... aah... aaah... CHOO!" came a hearty sneeze and the sides of the snowbank fell away, exposing a shivering Sassy. Simultaneously twin golden lights came on at either side of her as Angus and Edmond opened their eyes in the gathering dusk.

Sassy shook herself vigorously to get rid of any snow left on her coat and looked accusingly at Edmond.

A hearty sneeze made the walls of the snowbank fall away.

"I d-d-don't like this g-g-game," she said through chattering teeth. "I'm f-f-freezing-g-g. Diane will be very cross if I catch a cold."

"I'm sorry, Sassy," said Edmond, looking concerned. "I don't want you to get sick."

Angus walked over to show support for his little brother. "It's OK, you didn't mean any harm."

While Angus calmed Edmond and Savannah made a fuss over Sassy, all four heard a faint whimper coming from another nearby drift.

"Oh no! We forgot about Ellie!" Edmond cried.

He and Angus ran over and shoveled the snow away from the stoic little Dachshund.

"You told me to hide... but you didn't say for how long,"

said Ellie, shaking the remaining flakes off her gray, brown and black coat.

Thump... thump... Two snowballs hit the boys in the back and Sassy and Savannah jumped up and down with glee.

Ellie joined the girls, making it three against two. The lads took up the challenge and snowballs flew around the park until the five friends were laughing and out of breath.

It was almost dinner time and the friends had worked up a good appetite. They called a truce and went their separate ways, promising to set up another playdate soon.

CHAPTER 10

"Silent night, Holy night... all is calm... all is bright..."

Angus and Edmond sang, their sweet voices blending with those of other revelers on the classic yacht as it rocked gently in the dark waters of New York Harbor. They were snug and warm on a padded banquette in a heated solarium amid boughs of fragrant Balsam fir, sparkling decorations and strings of multi-colored lights.

They sipped hot cocoa with melted marshmallows and nibbled on cookies as a live band played during the 90-minute "Cocoa & Carols" cruise on board a 1920s style yacht that combined old world charm with advanced technologies -- teak decks, mahogany trim and carbon fiber rigging. The outing had appealed to the lads as an ideal way to get into the Christmas spirit.

For that special occasion, the brothers wore Scottish attire – a rugged but not too heavy kilt and traditional diced Glengarry hat with ribbons for the brawny Angus, and a tartan tam and formal Highland-wear trousers for Edmond's slim frame.

Between carols, Edmond hopped off the banquette

and carefully made his way along the polished deck of the swaying yacht. He found a suitable spot near a window from which he could take artful photos of the dazzling lights of the Manhattan skyline.

Meanwhile, Angus mingled with the other guests, who were toasting the season with a choice of beverage -- beer, wine or champagne. He saw a group that included the captain and a kilted gentleman, introduced himself and joined the conversation.

"I met some interesting folks," he later told Edmond.

"The captain told me that at this time of year, holiday cruises are very popular for office parties, wine tastings, brunch or private dinner charters, and Jazz concerts. The Classic Harbor Line operates out of four locations, and one of them is Key West! I need to alert our conch friends."

"Oh, yes. Remember the sunsets we watched from Mallory Square, Angus? They were so spectacular the tourists applauded. Imagine how amazing it would be to see a Key West sunset from the deck of a schooner!"

"And listen, bro, you'll never guess what else! I met a fellow Scot -- a Highlander named John Chisholm who, like me, is wearing a kilt. He and his wife, Christine, live in Edinburgh and are flying to Fort Lauderdale tomorrow to board a Caribbean Christmas cruise. They were very interested in hearing the story of our own Scottish roots."

"Did you ask if they know Jamie?"

"I did. They don't know him, but they promised to look him up and say 'hello' the next time they are in Inverness."

It was soon time to head back to Chelsea Piers. As the yacht approached the docks, the band played "Jingle Bells" and guests exchanged a flurry of holiday wishes while they lined up to disembark.

From the Harbor Line slip, it was a short distance to

the subway that would take the lads to Grand Central Station, only a few minutes' walk from their home.

* * *

Back in the Dicksons' apartment, Edmond continued to test his voice quality by emulating Freddie Mercury while Queen's greatest hits played in the background.

"*We-e-e* are the *champ*-ions, my *frie*-end," he sang. Then raising his imaginary mic, he struck a dramatic pose and turned to his brother.

"Angus, did you know Freddie Mercury loved cats? He had at least 10 – Tiffany, Oscar, Romeo, Delilah,

Miko, Dorothy, Tom, Jerry, Goliath and Lily. And he dedicated an album to 'all the cat lovers across the universe'! How much fun would it be to live with a rock star?"

Angus did not reply. He was staring intently at the cover of the New York by Rail magazine on the coffee table.

"Look! Look at this!" he held up the magazine, showing a photo of an ancient castle rising from a small island in the Hudson River.

"What is it?" Edmond paused in a mid-kick.

"It's an abandoned Scottish castle on Bannerman's Island in the Hudson Highlands."

"So?"

"Well, we are Scottish, and possibly of royal blood. When the weather warms up, we'll have to take the train up to Beacon and check it out. We'll need to find out if there's a MacBean-Bannerman or Dickson-Bannerman connection. It looks like a real fixer-upper, but, who knows, we might have some claim to it..."

Hearing the determination in his brother's voice, Edmond knew it was no use trying to dissuade him. With a deep sign of resignation, he strutted over to the Dicksons' PC to access felineage.com.

CPSIA information can be obtained
at www.ICGtesting.com
Printed in the USA
BVHW060429281121
622193BV00001B/1